THIS WALT DISNEY CLASSIC EDITION
BELONGS TO:

_____

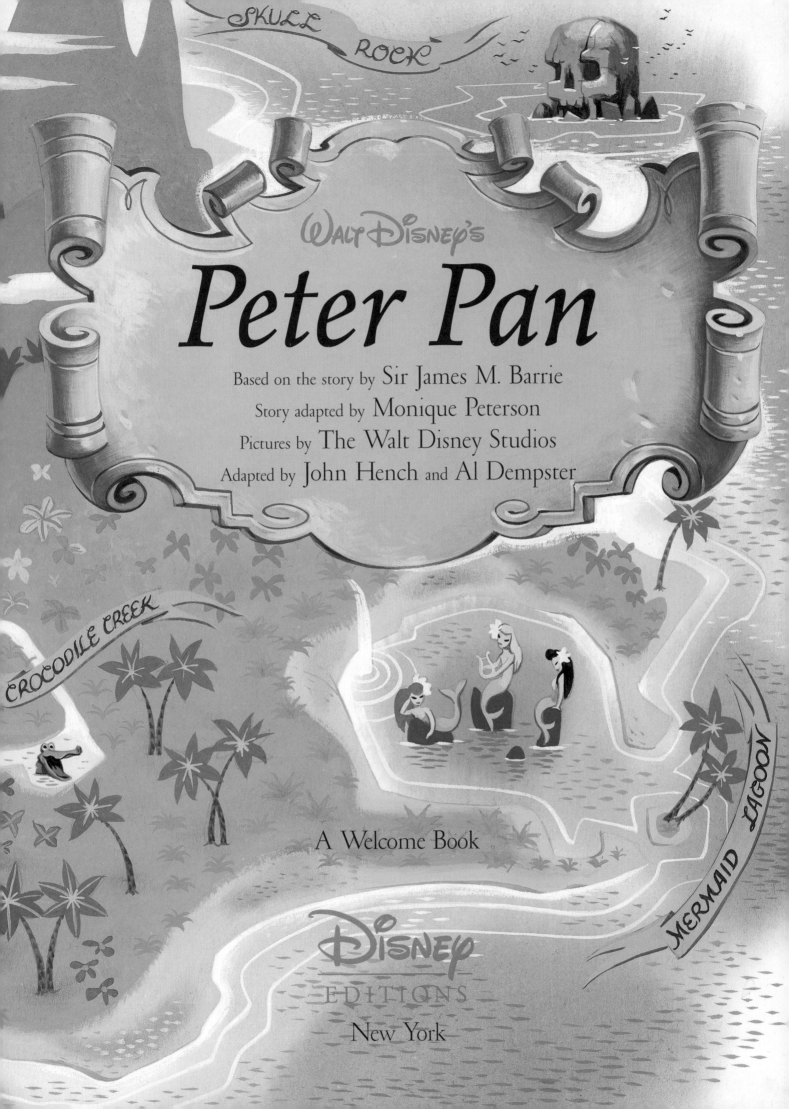

Walt Disney's
Peter Pan

Based on the story by Sir James M. Barrie

Story adapted by Monique Peterson

Pictures by The Walt Disney Studios

Adapted by John Hench and Al Dempster

A Welcome Book

DISNEY EDITIONS

New York

N estled away in the corner house of a quiet London street lived
Mother and Father Darling and their three children, Wendy,
Michael, and John. Nana the St. Bernard lived there, too. Nana
had the very important job of being the children's nursemaid.

Everyone's favorite hour of the day was just before bedtime. That's when
Wendy told stories about Peter Pan and Never Land.

Never Land was an enchanted place filled with beautiful mermaids,
magical fairies, brave Indians, and swashbuckling pirates. John and Michael
loved the pirates best of all and always enacted the slashing duels between Peter
Pan and his archenemy, Captain Hook.

Father Darling did not approve of such raucous play and blamed the trouble on Wendy's fantastical stories. "You're stuffing the boys' heads with absolute poppycock!" he scolded. "It's high time you had a room of your own! This will be your last night in the nursery!"

Wendy was not the only one whose days in the nursery were numbered. Father decided there would be no more dogs for nursemaids and tied up poor Nana outside in the garden. "The children aren't puppies, they're people," he explained to the brooding St. Bernard. "And sooner or later, the children have to grow up."

That night the children were very sad indeed.

Later that night, Peter Pan slipped in through the open window looking
for his lost shadow. Nana had nipped it off the night before when Peter Pan had
been sitting outside the window listening to Wendy's stories.

"I might have never seen you after tonight," Wendy told Peter Pan as she
sewed his shadow back on. "For I must grow up tomorrow."

"No!" shouted Peter Pan. "I won't have it! Come with me to Never Land.
You'll never grow up there!"

Peter Pan's fairy friend, Tinker Bell, had come, too. But she wasn't very
excited about Wendy coming to Never Land. She didn't like all the attention
Peter Pan gave Wendy.

Wendy, John, and Michael were eager to go. Except—they had to fly.

"It's easy!" Peter Pan said. "Just think of the most wonderful things . . . that and pixie dust, and it's like having wings!"

Before they knew it, the children were soaring out of the nursery window. Nana barked good-bye as they flew to the second star to the right and straight on till morning.

Meanwhile, in Pirate's Cove, Captain Hook was hopping mad. He'd wanted revenge ever since Peter had cut off his hand in a duel and tossed it to a crocodile—a crocodile that still follows Hook to this day, licking its chops for more. Fortunately for Captain Hook, the croc also swallowed an alarm clock and always warns him with a *tick-tock, tick-tock, tick-tock*.

Now, Captain Hook and his crew had combed the entire island for Peter's hideout and found nothing. But Captain Hook had a thought. "I'll bet the Indian chief's daughter knows where Pan is hiding," he snarled. "She knows the island better than I know me own ship."

Suddenly a shout came from the crow's nest. "Peter Pan, ahoy! Off the starboard bow!"

"What?" shouted Captain Hook as he peered through his spyglass. "Swoggle me eyes! It *is* Pan!" he sneered, spotting Peter Pan and the children on a cloud . . . like sitting ducks. "Pipe up the crew!" he bellowed.

Mr. Smee shouted, "All hands on deck!"

"We'll get him this time," Captain Hook said, curling his lips into a cruel grin. "Man the guns! Range forty-two . . . Elevation sixty-five . . . three degrees west . . . steady . . ."

Meanwhile, from the top of the cloud, Wendy, John, and Michael had the most wonderful view of Never Land.

"Look! It's the Mermaid Lagoon!" Wendy said excitedly.

"And the Indian encampment!" added John.

"Oh, look! Cap'n Hook and the pirates!" Michael noticed, just as . . .

KABLOOM!!! A cannonball ripped right through the clouds.

"Tinker Bell!" Peter shouted. "Take Wendy and the boys to the island. I'll fend off Captain Hook!"

So Wendy, John, and Michael followed Tinker Bell to the island. But Wendy couldn't fly quickly enough. "Not so fast, Tinker Bell! We can't keep up with you!" she shouted. But Tink didn't care. She sped off jealously ahead, losing Wendy and the boys through the clouds.

Tinker Bell raced through the Never Land tropical forest until she came to Hangman's Tree. With a quick hop and a jump, Tink bounced off an old toadstool and vaulted off a leaf straight into the secret opening of Peter Pan's hideout.

Deep in the underground cave, Tinker Bell found the Lost Boys snoozing away. She flitted about and rousted them out of their slumber.

"Ting-a-ling-a-ling! Ting-a-ling-a-ling!" chimed Tinker Bell.

"What!" cried the Lost Boys. "Orders from Peter Pan . . . shoot down a terrible Wendy bird?"

"Ting-a-ling-a-ling!" Tink nodded urgently.

"Let's go!" the boys shouted with excitement. And they grabbed clubs and bows and arrows and slingshots and pellet guns and scrambled out of Hangman's Tree.

"I see it!" called the oldest boy, pointing at Wendy's blue dress. "Ready! . . . Aim! . . . Fire!!"

The boys' flying rocks and arrows shattered Wendy's happy thoughts and she fell screaming down to the ground.

Luckily for Wendy, Peter Pan escaped the pirates and heard her scream just in the nick of time. He swiftly dove to the island and caught her, saving her life.

Tinker Bell fumed with envy.

"I did it! I did it!" the Lost Boys shouted, each taking credit for shooting down the Wendy bird.

Peter was not pleased at all. "You blockheads! I bring you a mother to tell you stories and you shoot her down!"

When the boys explained that they followed orders from Tinker Bell, Peter got even angrier. "Tinker Bell!" he shouted. "I charge you with high treason! I hereby banish you forever!"

And with that, Tink flew away in a huff.

"All right, men," Peter announced to the excited boys. "Go and capture some Indians. C'mon, Wendy, I'll show you the mermaids."

As Peter and Wendy flew off, John led the boys through the Never Land wilderness. They marched across the island, hopping over rocks and singing through the fields, until they spotted footprints.

"Aha!" cried John, trying his very best to be a worthy leader. "First we must surround them and then we'll take them by surpri—!"

WHOOP! The Never Land Indians ambushed the boys and carried them away to their camp.

The boys thought their capture was only a game—but the chief was furious. He thought they had kidnapped his daughter. If Tiger Lily wasn't back by sunset, he threatened to burn the boys at the stake.

At Mermaid Lagoon, Wendy saw real live mermaids with flowers in their hair.
"Would you like to meet them?" Peter asked, smiling.
"I'd love to!" Wendy replied, admiring their beauty.
But the mermaids weren't as thrilled to meet a *girl*.
"Who's *she*?" they quizzed. "What's *she* doing here?" And the spiteful mermaids swam around Wendy, splashing her with water.
Before they had a chance to pull her into the lagoon, Peter Pan heard a noise. "Shhh!!"

"It's Captain Hook!" Peter Pan whispered. The dastardly pirate and Mr. Smee were heading straight for Skull Rock. "And they've captured Tiger Lily!"

Quickly and quietly, Peter and Wendy followed them. When they got to Skull Rock, they saw Tiger Lily had been tied to an anchor, soon to be washed over with the incoming tide.

"This is the proposition," Hook threatened the Indian princess. "You tell me the hiding place of Peter Pan, and I shall set you free!"

But Tiger Lily refused to say a word.

"The Spirit of Mighty Sea Water speaks! Beware!" shouted Peter Pan, disguising his voice.

Captain Hook searched the rocks for the suspicious sound. Peter spoke again, this time pretending to be Hook: "Smee! Release the princess! Bring her back to her people!"

But Hook caught Peter and nearly stabbed him with his sword. The two fought the most fearsome duel along the cliffs of Skull Rock. Peter Pan defeated Captain Hook just in time to save Tiger Lily!

With Tiger Lily in his arms, Peter Pan flew straight to the Indian encampment. Wendy trailed behind.

The chief was overjoyed. He freed the boys and made Peter Chief Flying Eagle. Everyone started dancing and singing and drumming—everyone, that is, except Wendy. She had to gather firewood while Peter danced with Tiger Lily.

That's when Wendy finally decided Never Land wasn't so wonderful after all. "I'm going home!" she said, and stormed off.

Meanwhile, back at the pirate ship, Captain Hook heard that Peter Pan had banished Tinker Bell. So he ordered Smee to capture Tink.

"Miss Bell," Hook declared, "I'm admitting defeat, and tomorrow I leave. I brought you here to tell Peter Pan I bear him no ill will." Then, more sweetly, he said, "Rumor has it that Wendy has come between you and Peter Pan."

Tinker Bell sulked.

"Then it's true!" Captain Hook wailed. "I have an idea! We'll sail tomorrow and take Wendy with us!"

Tinker Bell twittered her wings happily.

"But we don't know where Peter Pan lives," noted Smee.

"Ting-a-ling-a-ling!" The glowing sprite flew eagerly to the map. She flitted over Peg Leg Point . . . Blind Man's Bluff . . . Crocodile Creek. But only after Captain Hook agreed not to lay a finger or a hook on Peter Pan did Tinker Bell show him Hangman's Tree.

"Thank you, my dear," Captain Hook said with a smile. Then he locked her shut in the lantern.

MOUNTAINS   BOG   HANGMAN'S TREE

After the boys came back to the hideout, Wendy tucked her brothers into bed. She told them wonderful stories about home and mother. Before they knew it, everyone was terribly homesick. Even the Lost Boys wanted to go home with them.

Peter Pan scoffed at the idea. "Go on! But once you're grown up you can never come back!" And he turned his back as the children waved good-bye and climbed out of the hideout.

Right outside Hangman's Tree, Captain Hook and his buccaneers waited . . . skulking in the shadows. As each boy popped out of the tree, the pirates snatched them up one by one and tied them up with ropes. Wendy was the last to come out. She didn't even have a chance to scream before they covered her mouth and tied her up, too.

Then Captain Hook delivered a special present to Peter Pan marked *from Wendy*. It was really a bomb set to go off any minute. "I promised not to lay a finger or a hook on Peter Pan!" Captain Hook said with a wicked laugh. "And the captain *never* breaks his promise!"

A frightful fate awaited Wendy and the boys once on board the pirate
ship. "Sign up as a pirate," Captain Hook warned, "or walk the plank!!"

The boys scrambled to sign their names in Captain Hook's book. But
Wendy put a quick stop to that.

"Aren't you ashamed of yourselves!" she scolded in her most motherly
voice. "Peter Pan will save us!"

Captain Hook cackled. "You see, we left a present for Peter . . ." And he
told how Peter Pan would be blasted out of Never Land forever.

But Wendy stood firm. "We will never join your ship!"

"Very well." Hook gestured to the long wooden board. "Ladies first!"

As Wendy bravely walked the plank, Tinker Bell broke out of the lantern cage and sped off to save Peter Pan from the bomb.

Then, while the tearful boys watched, Wendy jumped. Everyone waited for the splash—but heard nothing.

The pirates thought the ship was bewitched, but it was Peter Pan—he had flown back in time to save Wendy!

"You're next, Hook!" shouted Peter Pan as he swooped onto the ship and set the boys free. The boys climbed up to the crow's nest, fending off the nasty pirates while Peter Pan took on Hook.

In the most exciting duel ever, Peter agreed not to fly—he would fight Captain Hook man to man. They fenced high along the rigging, and Peter narrowly escaped Hook's blade many times. But at the very end, Peter knocked the pirate's sword away. Hook surrendered, agreeing to leave Never Land forever.

So Captain Hook and his crew sailed the dinghy into the horizon with the *tick-tock, tick-tock* of the croc licking its chops close behind.

"Heave those halyards! Hoist the anchor!" shouted Peter Pan as the new captain of Hook's ship. "We're sailing off to London!"

"Hooray to Cap'n Pan!" shouted the Lost Boys as they followed Peter's orders.

"John, Michael, we're going home!" Wendy cheered.

The best part of all was when Tinker Bell sprinkled the entire ship with pixie dust! The golden ship floated up into the sky and sailed off into the starry night. They sailed all the way back to the Darling house and through the open nursery window, where Peter returned them safe and sound.

Peter Pan bid the children farewell, taking the Lost Boys with him—for they weren't quite ready to grow up. And Wendy, John, and Michael waved good-bye as their friends sailed across the moon to Never Land, where you can still visit them today.